MERCER MAYER'S LITTLE CRITTER

I SMELL CHRISTMAS

To Trip, Willy and Nate

A MERCER MAYER LTD. / J. R. SANSEVERE BOOK

MERCER MAYER'S LITTLE CRITTER book, characters, text and images © 1997 Mercer Mayer.
LITTLE CRITTER is a registered trademark of Orchard House Licensing Company.
MERCER MAYER'S LITTLE CRITTER and MERCER MAYER'S LITTLE CRITTER LOGO are trademarks of Orchard House Licensing Company.
Published in the United States by Inchworm Press, an imprint of GT Publishing Corporation.
For information, address Inchworm Press, 16 East 40th Street, New York, NY 10016.
Printed in Malaysia.

inchworm PRESS

It is almost Christmas.
We go to get our Christmas tree.
Dad picks a big one. Mom picks a small one.
Little Sister and I pick the best one of all.

When we get home, I help Dad set up the tree.
The tree is crooked, so I give it a little push.
Uh-oh! Watch out, Dad!

Mom makes hot chocolate.
Little Sister drinks a little cup because she is little.
I drink a big cup because I am big.

We all decorate the tree.
But Dad always puts the star on top.
We hang candy canes, but we eat some, too.

We go shopping for
Christmas presents.
Then we get ice cream.

On Christmas Eve, Grandma
and Grandpa come over for dinner.
They bring Grandma's famous apple pie.

"Merry Christmas, Grandma and Grandpa!"
I say and give them both a kiss.

We have a big turkey dinner.

Then we sing Christmas carols.
And drink Dad's yummy eggnog
with cinnamon on top.

Then it is time for bed.
Little Sister and I leave cookies for Santa.
They are ginger snaps, Little Sister's favorite.

FOR
SANTA
LOVE US.

I toss and turn, trying to fall asleep.
I wonder if Santa will like the cookies, but mostly
I wonder what I am going to get for Christmas.

The next morning, there are lots
of presents under the tree.

I get the baseball mitt I always wanted
and the biggest lollipop in the world!